The Spooky Scavenger Hunt

Based on the television series created by Craig Bartlett

Grosset & Dunlap
An Imprint of Penguin Group (USA) Inc.

™ and © 2011 The Jim Henson Company. JIM HENSON'S mark & logo, DINOSAUR TRAIN mark & logo, characters and elements are trademarks of The Jim Henson Company. All Rights Reserved. Published by Grosset & Dunlap, a division of Penguin Young Readers Group, 345 Hudson Street, New York, New York 10014. GROSSET & DUNLAP is a trademark of Penguin Group (USA) Inc. Manufactured in China.

The PBS KIDS logo is a registered mark of the Public Broadcasting Service and is used with permission.

http://pbskids.org/dinosaurtrain

ISBN 978-0-448-45604-1   10 9 8 7 6 5 4 3 2

W9-APV-381

The wind was blowing. There was a full moon. It was the perfect night for a spooky scavenger hunt.

"Three tickets for the Night Train, please," Mr. Pteranodon said.

"Just three? Where's the rest of the family?" asked the station manager.

"Don was going to come, but he fell asleep," said Tiny.

"And *no way* would Shiny come on a spooky scavenger hunt!" said Buddy.

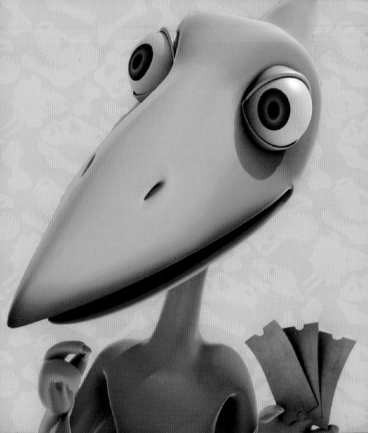

The station manager leaned out of his window. "You're very lucky, Buddy and Tiny," he said. "We only do this ride on *really* spooky nights!"

Toot-toot! The Dinosaur Train pulled into the station. *"Mwah-ha-ha. Good eeee-vening,"* the conductor said as he opened the door. "Welcome to the Night Train!"

Everyone boarded the train and took their seats.
"Boy, it's dark out," said Buddy. "I'm glad you're with me, Tiny."
"Don't worry, Buddy. We'll be fine," Tiny told him.

"That's right," said Mr. Pteranodon. "Just stick with me. *Nothing* scares me!"

Suddenly, the conductor popped up behind Mr. Pteranodon. *"Mwah-ha-ha,"* he shouted.

But Mr. Pteranodon wasn't scared.

"That didn't even scare you a little,
Mr. Pteranodon?" asked the conductor.
"Well, the Big Pond is plenty spooky.
Especially for dinosaurs who don't have
night vision!"

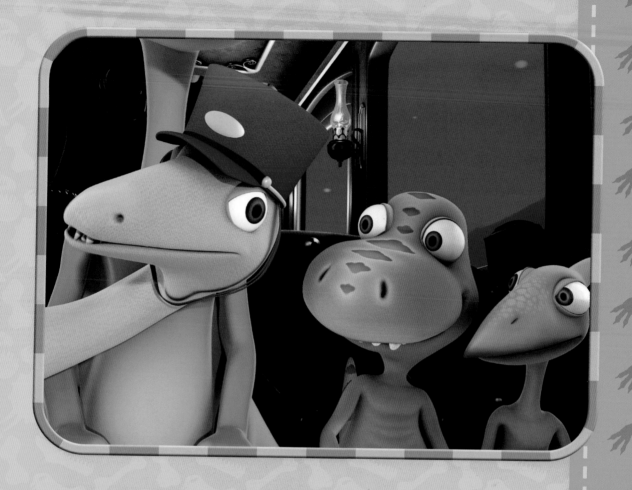

"What's night vision?" Buddy asked.

"That's a good question," said the conductor.
"We Troodons have eyes that can see in the dark.
It's how we hunt. We're nocturnal. That means we
look for food at night!"

"We Pteranodons look for *our* food—fish—during the day!" Tiny said.

"Hunting at night is easy when you have eyeshine," the conductor said. He snapped his fingers and the lights went out.

"Nocturnal animals have eyes that glow, like mine!" said the conductor. "It helps us find one another in the dark. And speaking of the dark, it's time to go on our spooky scavenger hunt!"

Everyone got off the train.

"Boy, am I glad you're here. Can I stick with you?" a voice said.

Buddy and Tiny turned around and saw their friend Ned Brachiosaurus.

"Of course you can, Ned. You'll be safe with us," said Mr. Pteranodon.

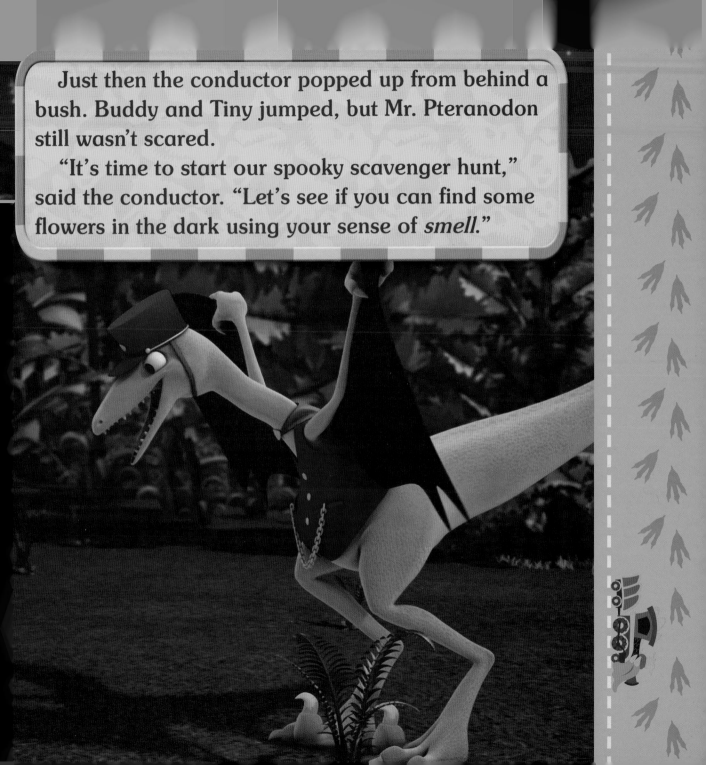

Just then the conductor popped up from behind a bush. Buddy and Tiny jumped, but Mr. Pteranodon still wasn't scared.

"It's time to start our spooky scavenger hunt," said the conductor. "Let's see if you can find some flowers in the dark using your sense of *smell*."

"I bet you can find some, Buddy," Tiny said. "T. rexes have a great sense of smell!"

"You're right! Come on, everybody. Follow my nose!" Buddy said.

Buddy, Tiny, Ned, and Mr. Pteranodon set off to find some flowers.

"I just smell leaves and dirt," said Tiny.

Ned sniffed around. "My nose is kinda stuffed up tonight," he said. "Do you smell anything, Buddy?"

"I smell flowers! This way," Buddy shouted. Buddy led the group to a patch of flowers. *"Ta-da!"* he said.

"Great job, Buddy," the conductor said as he popped out of the flowers. "Next up, see if you can use your *hearing* to find a frog. They have very loud croaks!"

The conductor held up a picture of the kind of frog they were looking for.

"We know a frog!" said Tiny. "Her name is Patricia. She likes to hunt bugs near the water at night!"

Buddy, Tiny, Ned, and Mr. Pteranodon walked down to the water.

"Do you hear anything, Buddy?" Ned asked.

"I hear insects," said Buddy.

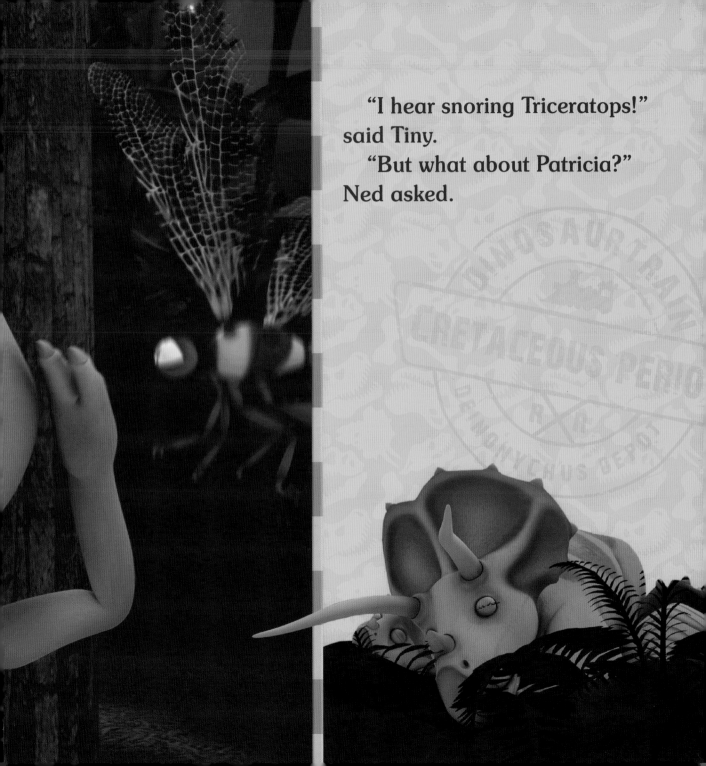

"I hear snoring Triceratops!" said Tiny.

"But what about Patricia?" Ned asked.

Ribbit. Ribbit. There was a loud sound behind the bushes and a frog hopped out. "Hello, Buddy. Hello, Tiny," Patricia the frog said.

"Great job," said the conductor, peering
out of the bushes. "You used your hearing
to find Patricia!"

"There's just one more thing to find on our spooky scavenger hunt," said the conductor. "See if you can use your *eyes* to find another creature by spotting their eyeshine!"

Buddy, Tiny, Ned, Mr. Pteranodon, and the conductor started to walk through the woods. "Look at that huge dinosaur!" Buddy said and pointed in front of them.

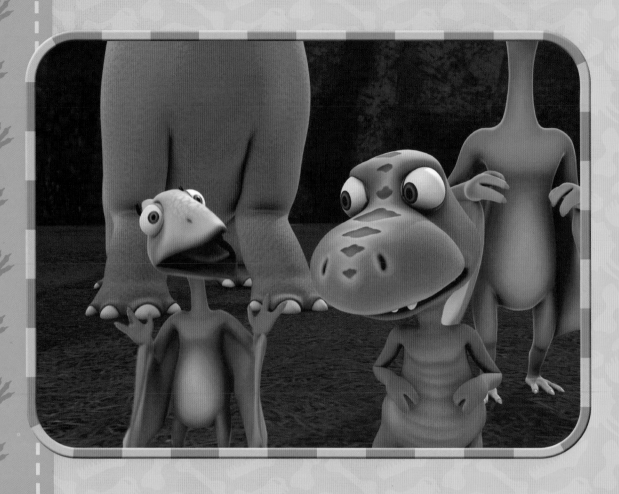

"Oh, Buddy," said Tiny. "What an imagination. It's just a tree!"

"Phew. That was spooky," said Ned.

Suddenly, Tiny screamed. There were two eyes peering out of the bushes at her!

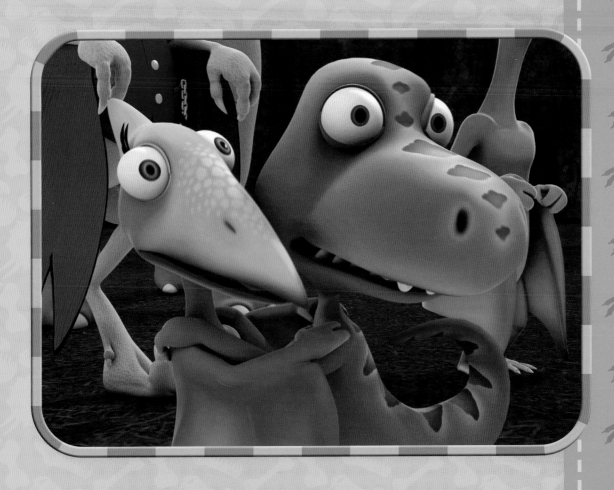

Tiny and Buddy held on to each other.
"What *is* that?" Buddy asked.
"Maybe it's Mr. Conductor trying to
spook us again," said Tiny.
"Not this time," said the conductor. "I'm
right here!"

"We'll go check it out," said Mr. Pteranodon. "That's right," said the conductor. "Nothing scares us!"

Mr. Pteranodon and the conductor walked over to the bush. The eyes blinked at them.

Just then, the creature jumped out at them. They both screamed, and the conductor jumped into Mr. Pteranodon's arms!

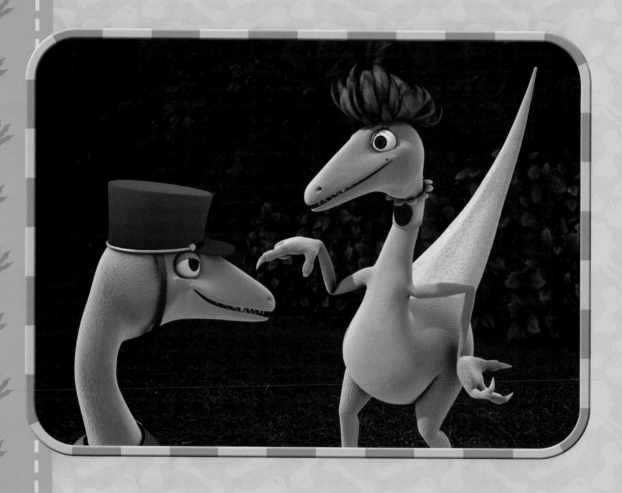

"It's the conductor's mom!" shouted Buddy and Tiny.

"What are you doing here in the dark?" the conductor asked his mom.

"I'm hunting for food, of course," she said. "What are *you* doing out here?"

"We're on a spooky scavenger hunt!" said Tiny.
"Why, of course you are," said the conductor's
mom. "Do you know my favorite part of the
spooky scavenger hunt? The Troodon show on
the Night Train. Let's go!"

Everyone got back on the train and took their seats. The Troodons surrounded Buddy and Tiny and started to sing.

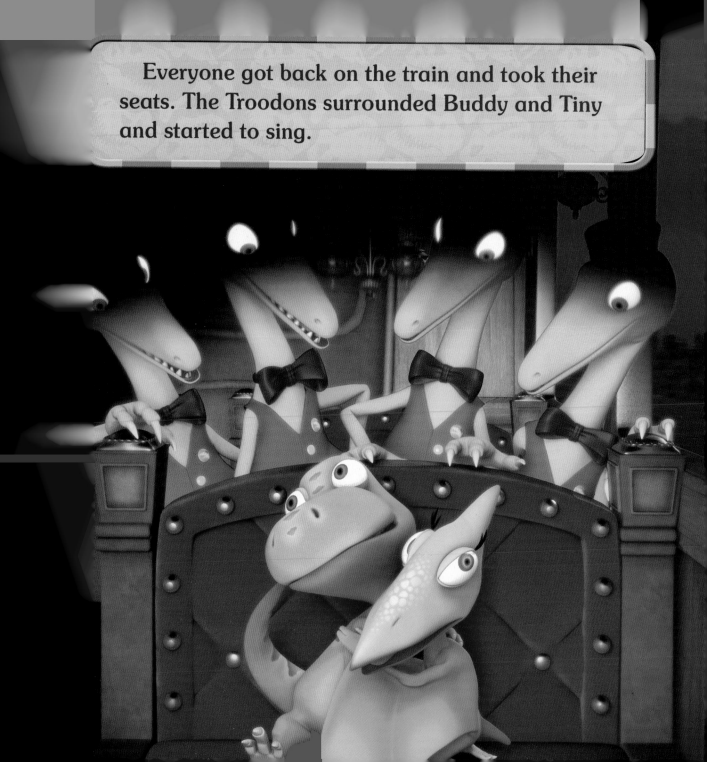

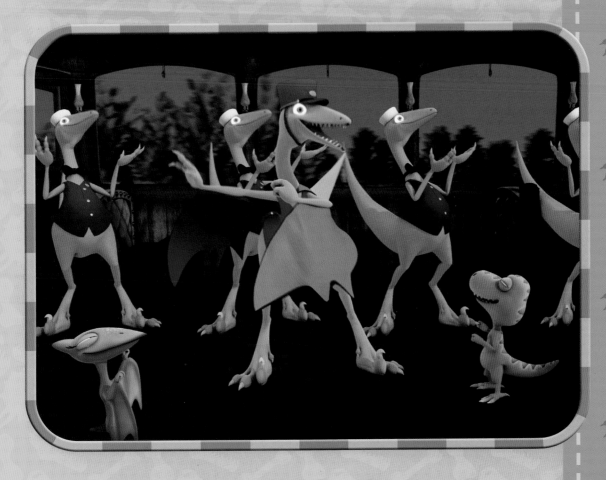

Soon everyone joined in. It was a party
on the Night Train!

The show ended and everyone went outside on the deck to watch the stars as the Dinosaur Train sped away into the night.